PZ7.G296 T5 1985

Geringer, Laura.

A three hat day /

    c1985.

A THREE
HAT DAY

LAURA GERINGER

A THREE
HAT DAY

PICTURES BY
ARNOLD LOBEL

 HarperCollins*Publishers*

130201

Library of Congress Cataloging-in-Publication Data
Geringer, Laura.
    A three hat day.
    Summary: A hat collector is having a very bad day
until he meets his true love in the hat section of the
department store.
    1. Children's stories, American. [1. Hats—Fiction]
I. Lobel, Arnold, ill. II. Title.
PZ7.G296Th 1985   [E]   85-42640
ISBN 0-06-021988-2
ISBN 0-06-021989-0 (lib. bdg.)
ISBN 0-06-443157-6 (pbk.)

For Tony

R.R. Pottle the Third loved hats.

He loved fur hats
and firemen's helmets
and felt hats with feathers
tucked in the bands.
He loved top hats
and tiny hats.
He loved silk hats
and straw hats
and sailor hats.
He loved berets
and bonnets
and bathing caps
and bowlers.

R.R. Pottle was the last of a long line of Pottles.
Father collected canes.

Mother liked umbrellas.

Together they took long walks in the rain.

After a happy life together, Mother and Father died.

R.R. lived by himself in the Pottle mansion.

He was rather lonely.

He dreamed of meeting his future wife in the rain.

And he dreamed she would be wearing the perfect hat.

Every morning, when R.R. woke,
the first thing he did—before he polished his glasses,
before he combed his moustache
and his few strands of hair,
even before he yawned—
was choose a hat.

Sometimes,
when he was feeling sad,
he chose two
and wore them,
one on top of the other.
One bright, clear morning,
R.R. felt so sad
he wore *three* hats.
Marching down the street,
he passed two snakes
out for a sunny stroll
beneath a ginkgo tree.
R.R. noticed a cloud
hovering just above his head.

He passed two bluebirds
doing a fancy waltz in midair.
R.R. trudged on.
The cloud grew bigger and darker.

He passed two frogs in a pond,

singing a tender duet.

R.R. recognized the tune.

It was "Estrellita Be Mine," the love song.

R.R.'s shoulders drooped.

He heard thunder in the distance.

There was only one thing left to do
on such a glum day.
With a sigh of relief,
he glided through the revolving doors
of the largest hat store in town.

WHAT HATS!

There were fezzes and face veils,
tiaras and tam-o'-shanters.
There were sombreros and skullcaps,
pillboxes and panamas.

There were beanies with propellers.
There were derbies with green glitter
that glowed in the dark.
And much more.

R.R. began to zigzag in and out among the hats.

His spirits rose.

He tried on the fez and twirled his moustache.

He tried on the derby

and struck a devil-may-care pose.

He tried on the sombrero

and did a little jig.

The pom-poms

hit his nose.

"What are you DOING?"
a sharp voice rang out.
R.R. was doing a pirouette.
An angry saleswoman
pointed at him, scowling.
"STOP that!" she said.

R.R. blinked and shook his head.

He thought he hadn't heard right.

It was clear she didn't like him.

But why?

R.R. took off the sombrero,

slipped it back on the shelf, and backed away.

Tears came to his eyes. He turned to leave.

Just then, a round figure

rushed out from behind a curtain.

She wore a dress that hung like an apple sack,

a lopsided apron, and squeaky shoes.

When she saw R.R., she smiled.

It was the sweetest smile he had ever seen.

And above the smile was a hat. A *perfect* hat!

On one side, a sequin seal balanced

a shining ball on the tip of its nose.

On the other, tiny gold bells jangled.

And a plume as soft and gray as fog

graced the peak.

"Oh, Isabel," the cross one said.

"That little man is messing up our hats.

Look! He's wearing three—

one on top of the other!"

"Little man!" thought R.R., squaring his shoulders.

But Isabel was still smiling broadly at him.

"Why, Ida," she said, "we don't sell sailor hats."

She stepped up to R.R.

and gently took off

his sailor hat.

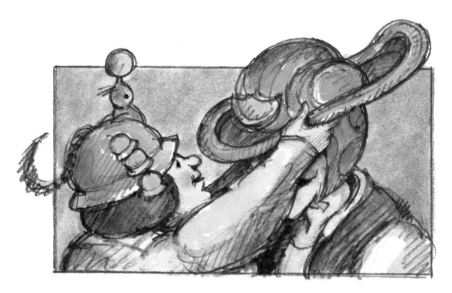

"And Ida," she said,

"we don't sell firemen's helmets."

And gently, she took off his helmet.

"And Ida, dear, we don't sell

bathing caps either." And gently, gently,

she took off R.R.'s bathing cap.

"It's clear," said Isabel, balancing on her toes,

"that this man is no messer-upper of hats.

"It's *very* clear," said she,

balancing R.R.'s three hats in her arms,

"that this man is a...lover of hats!"

And she beamed.

R.R. took off his glasses
and polished them with his handkerchief.
He cleared his throat. "Shall we go for a walk?"
he asked softly. "It's raining, I believe,"
and he held out his hand.

"Yes," said Isabel, taking it.

They passed a pond where two frogs sat doing a duet.

Isabel recognized the tune. It was "Love, Is That You?"

R.R. and Isabel hummed along

as they danced down the road.

And so,

Isabel and R.R. Pottle the Third

lived ever after in the Pottle mansion

where...

R.R. Pottle the Fourth was born.

R.R. Pottle the Fourth
did not like hats.
She did not like umbrellas—
and canes left her cold.

R.R. Pottle the Fourth loved shoes.